Why Tree Frog Sings at Night

by Jake Harris
illustrated by Stuart Billington

Harcourt
SCHOOL PUBLISHERS

Printed in Mexico

ISBN 10: 0-15-351437-X
ISBN 13: 978-0-15-351437-1

Ordering Options
ISBN 10: 0-15-351212-1 (Grade 2 Advanced Collection)
ISBN 13: 978-0-15-351212-4 (Grade 2 Advanced Collection)
ISBN 10: 0-15-358072-0 (package of 5)
ISBN 13: 978-0-15-358072-7 (package of 5)

1 2 3 4 5 6 7 8 9 10   050   15 14 13 12 11 10 09 08 07 06

The little, golden tree frog likes to sing at night. Its bright, little song can be heard on warm, damp summer nights. It is as much a part of darkness as are the stars in the sky.

Long ago, though, little Tree Frog's *chirrup-chirrup-chirrup* was only heard during the day. It was not at all welcomed by the other animals that lived in the pond.

"Who told Tree Frog that he could sing all day?" majestic Gray Heron would moan. "That racket ruffles my feathers. Tree Frog! Please stop that noise!"

"Would someone tell Tree Frog to take a nap?" wailed Dragonfly. "That croak of his is enough to make me fly away and find a new home. Why should I budge from the pond?" Dragonfly flew to the far side of the water, his wings twitching.

"There's no peace on the pond with Tree Frog making his terrible noise," said Duck. "Even the other frogs go scampering away when they hear him. Whoever told Tree Frog that he could sing has made a great mistake."

Still Tree Frog thought that his voice was beautiful. "I sing more sweetly than the forest birds," he said. "My songs are fit for kings and queens."

"I am the envy of everyone," bragged
Tree Frog. "Why, if all the other pond animals
had voices like mine, what a choir we would
make together!"

"Tree Frog's songs aren't fit for *anyone* to hear," the pond animals said to one another. "It is a great pity, but one of us will have to tell him the truth."

"Then the task is up to me," said Duck calmly.

When Tree Frog heard what Duck had to
say, he burst into tears. He was weighed down
with such sadness that he cried pitifully all
day and into the night.

It was Moon who later made the sad discovery of poor Tree Frog sobbing. Moon took pity on him. "What is the matter, Tree Frog?" Moon asked kindly.

Tree Frog peered up at Moon. "The pond animals do not enjoy my singing during the day," he wept. "They want me to stop."

Moon was filled with pity. "Why," said Moon, "if the pond animals do not like your singing during the day, then you must sing for me at night. I am often lonely in the darkest hours, and your voice will keep me company."

Tree Frog was overcome with joy. That is why now, while the pond animals sleep soundly, he sings the entire night long. His singing is so soft that it does not wake anyone.

Thanks to Moon, every night, Tree Frog
performs his songs on a silver stage.

Think Critically

1. What do you think "the silver stage" is that Tree Frog sang on at the end of the book?

2. If you were Tree Frog, how would you have felt when Duck told you your songs were no good?

3. Why did Tree Frog start to sing at night?

4. What words would you use to tell about Moon?

5. Would you change the ending of this story? How?

 Language Arts

Write a Letter Write a letter from Moon thanking Tree Frog for keeping her company and singing for her.

School-Home Connection Share the story *Why Tree Frog Sings at Night* with a family member. Talk about other animals that come out at night.